# THE JELLYBEANS
## and the Big Art Adventure

BY LAURA NUMEROFF AND NATE EVANS

ILLUSTRATED BY LYNN MUNSINGER

Abrams Books for Young Readers, New York

The illustrations in this book were made
with watercolor on paper.

Cataloging-in-Publication Data has been applied for and may be obtained
from the Library of Congress.
ISBN: 978-1-4197-0171-9

Text copyright © 2012 Laura Numeroff and Nate Evans
Illustrations copyright © 2012 Lynn Munsinger

Book design by Chad W. Beckerman

Printed and bound in China
10 9 8 7 6 5 4 3 2 1

Abrams Books for Young Readers are available at special discounts when purchased in quantity for
premiums and promotions as well as fundraising or educational use. Special editions can also be created
to specification. For details, contact specialsales@abramsbooks.com or the address below.

# ABRAMS
THE ART OF BOOKS SINCE 1949
115 West 18th Street
New York, NY 10011
www.abramsbooks.com

To Larry—Thank you for all your love and support
—L.N.

For the sweet and wonderfully talented
Jellybeans team—Laura Numeroff,
Lynn Munsinger, and Tamar Brazis—
with thanks
—N.E.

Bitsy loved to paint.

She painted while eating breakfast.

She painted while playing at the beach.

She even painted while bowling.

Bitsy liked showing her paintings to her best friends, Emily, Anna, and Nicole.

Emily loved to dance.

Anna loved to read.

And Nicole loved to play soccer.

Their favorite place to hang out was Petunia's, where
they loved to share their favorite candy—jellybeans.

Just as jellybeans are different flavors but go well together, the girls were all different but got along great—and so they called themselves the Jellybeans, too.

The girls met at Petunia's, and Bitsy pulled out her latest creation.

"That's a great painting," said Nicole, balancing a soccer ball on her head.

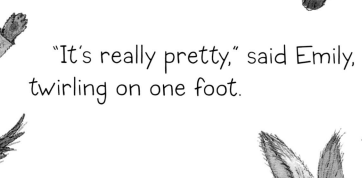

"It's really pretty," said Emily, twirling on one foot.

"It's dazzling," said Anna. "*Dazzling* is my new favorite word."

Mrs. Petunia Dinkley-Sneezer, the candy shop's
owner, came over to get a better look.
"My goodness," she said. "That *is* dazzling!"

"Bitsy can paint anything," said Nicole.

"That's perfect," said Mrs. Petunia Dinkley-Sneezer, "because I'm redecorating my shop and there's a wonderful way for Bitsy to help."

Mrs. Petunia Dinkley-Sneezer led the girls outside. "Bitsy, this is where I would like you to create something special."

"It's just a wall," said Emily.
"But it's like a big blank piece of paper," said Bitsy.
"And we're going to paint something amazing on it!"

"We?" asked Anna. "I don't know how to paint!"
"Me, neither," said Emily.
"All I can draw is a stick figure," Nicole said.
"Don't worry. Everyone can make something beautiful," said Bitsy. "I'll show you!"

Bitsy took the Jellybeans to a big museum. It was filled with all kinds of art.

Emily saw beautiful paintings.

EDGAR DOGAS

Anna stared at a huge statue.

Nicole loved the ancient art that was thousands of years old.

After visiting the museum, the Jellybeans
were excited to create their own art!

The next morning, Mrs. Petunia Dinkley-Sneezer
gave the girls paints and brushes and smocks.

Nicole painted flowers!

Emily painted a rainbow!

And Anna painted large, colorful letters!

"Now it's your turn," Emily said to Bitsy.

"What am I going to paint?" Bitsy wondered.

She stood in front of the wall all afternoon and didn't paint a thing.

"What's wrong?" asked Anna.
"Everyone will see this painting," Bitsy cried.
"What if nobody likes it?"

"Everyone will love it!" said Nicole.
"It's going to be a masterpiece," said Anna.
"We know you can do it!" said Emily.

Bitsy thought for a moment, and then she announced, "I have an idea!"

Bitsy picked up a paintbrush and started to paint.

The next day, Bitsy raced into Petunia's candy shop.
"The mural is finished," she shouted happily.

"I can't wait to see what you've done," said Mrs. Petunia Dinkley-Sneezer.

She and Bitsy walked outside. The other Jellybeans crowded around them.

"It's amazing!" said Emily.

"It's perfect!" said Nicole.
"It's dazzling!" cried Anna.
"What a beautiful mural," Mrs. Dinkley-Sneezer
said. "And I know just how to thank all of
you. Here is a treat as sweet as you are . . ."

# JELLYBEANS!